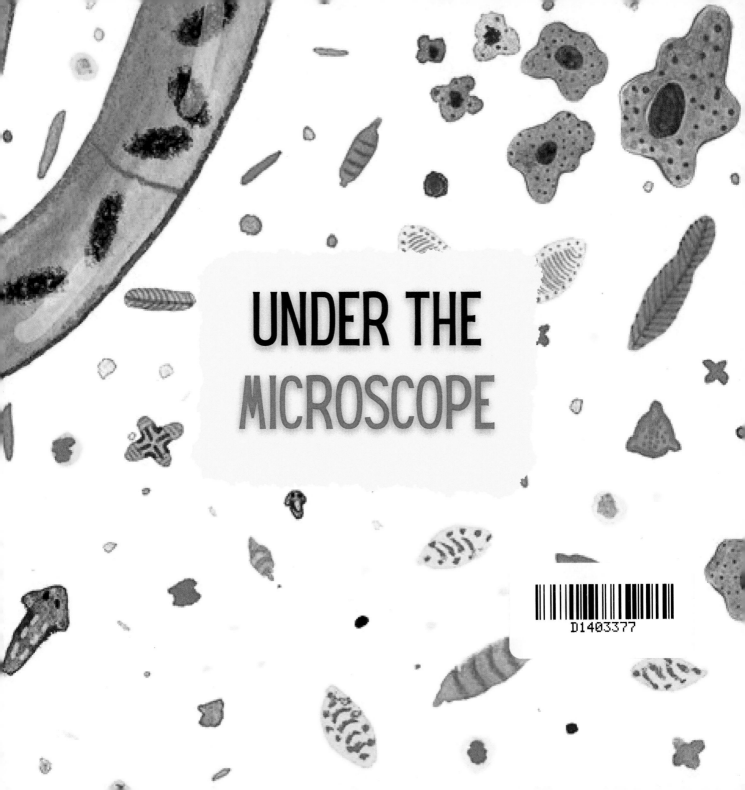

UNDER THE
MICROSCOPE

From the pond...

To the lab...

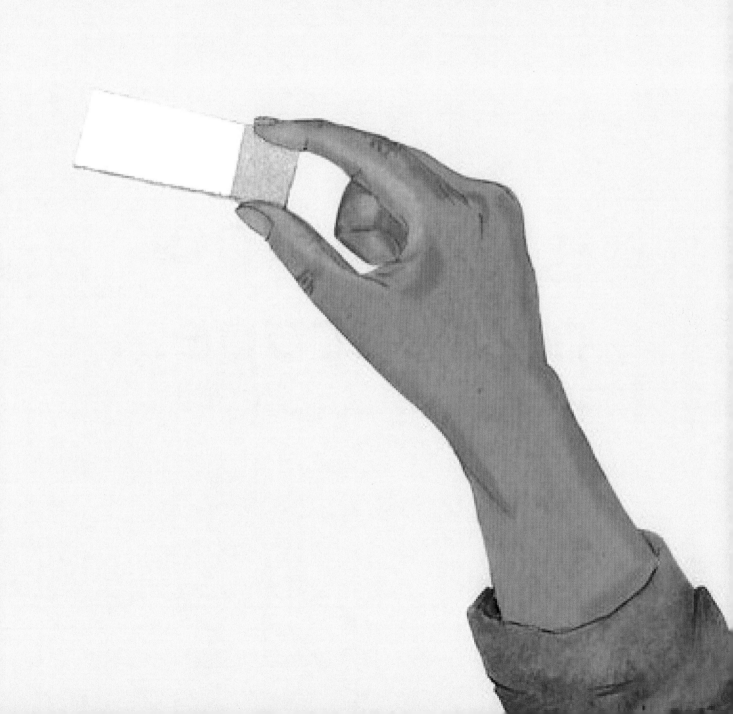

Under the microscope...

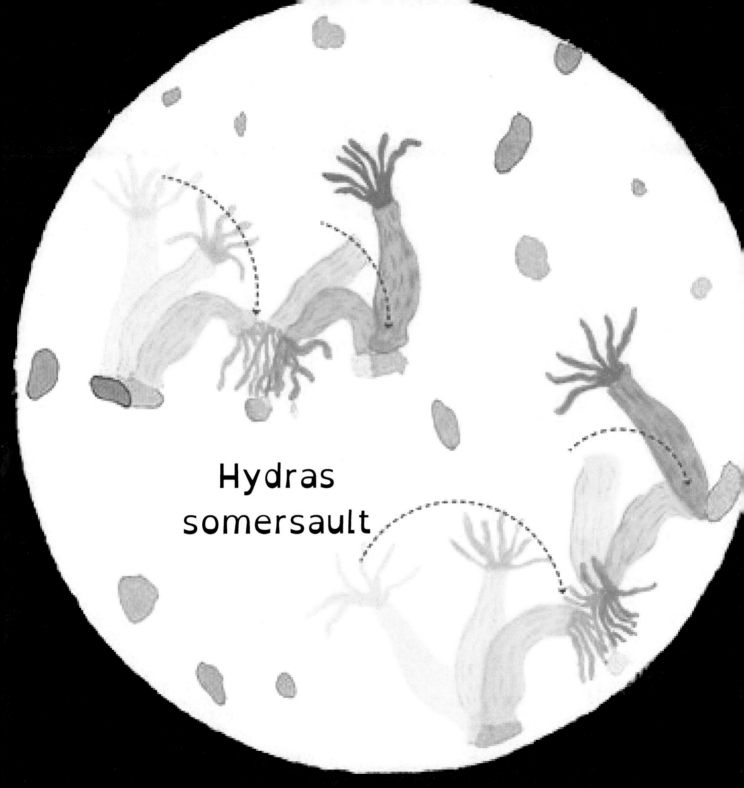

Hydras somersault

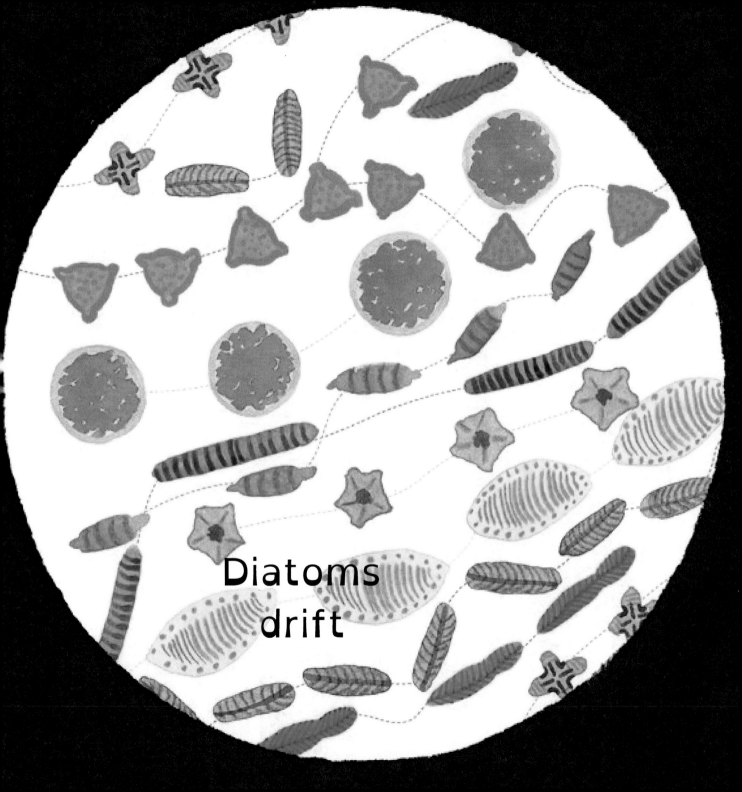

Euglenas
twist and turn

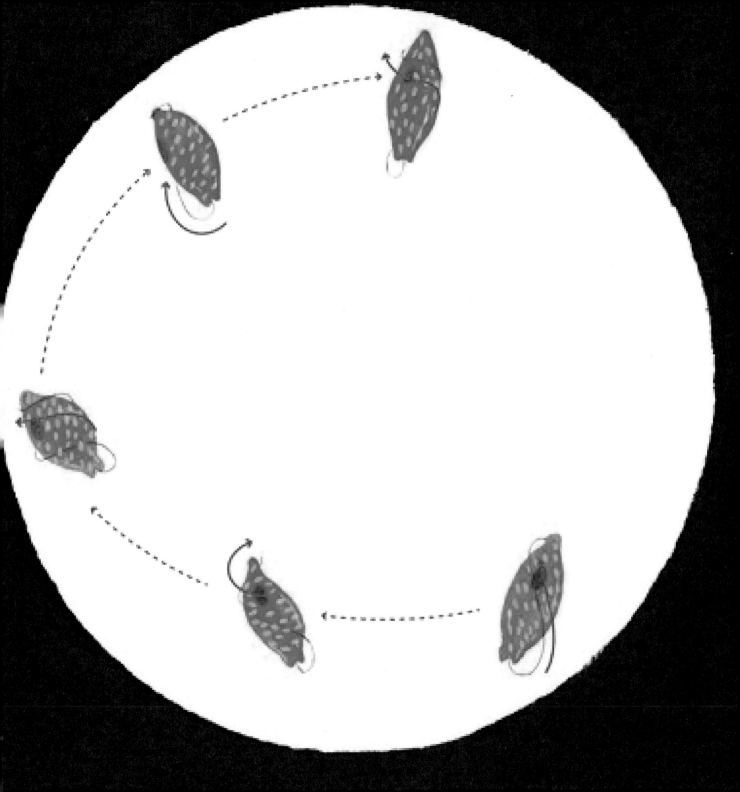

Under the microscope...

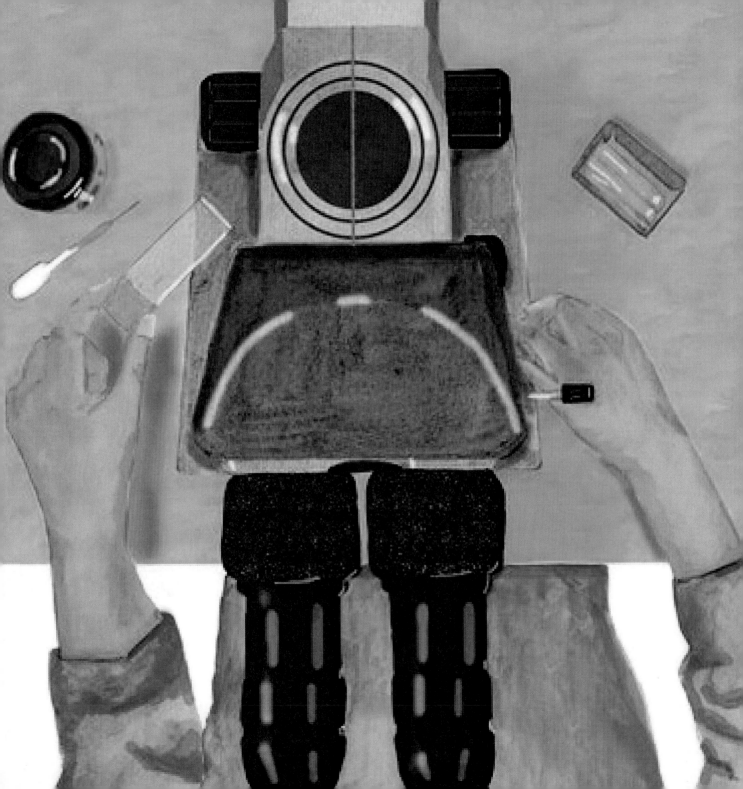

Planerias glide

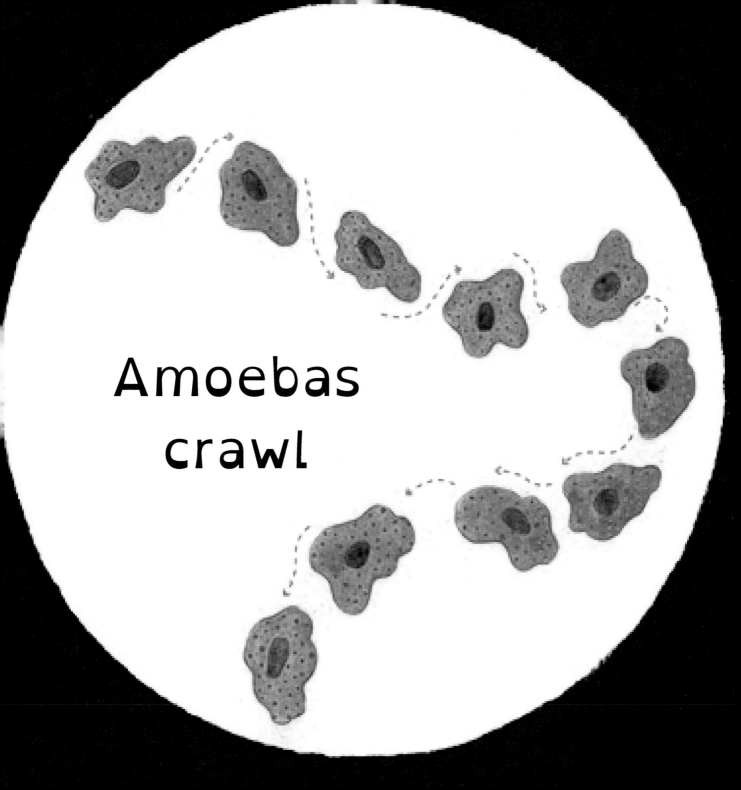

Copepods swim

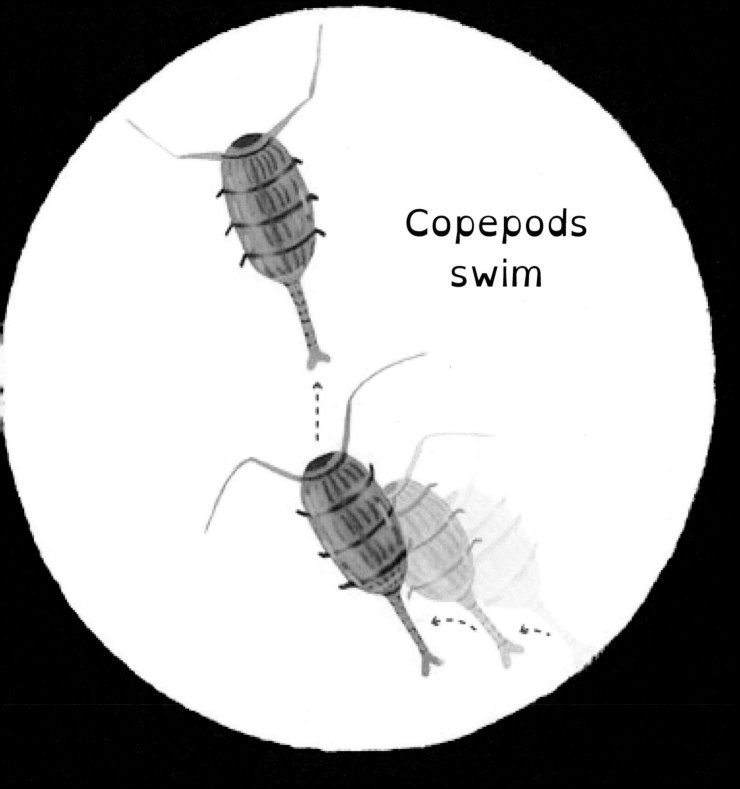

Copepods
swim

Under the microscope...

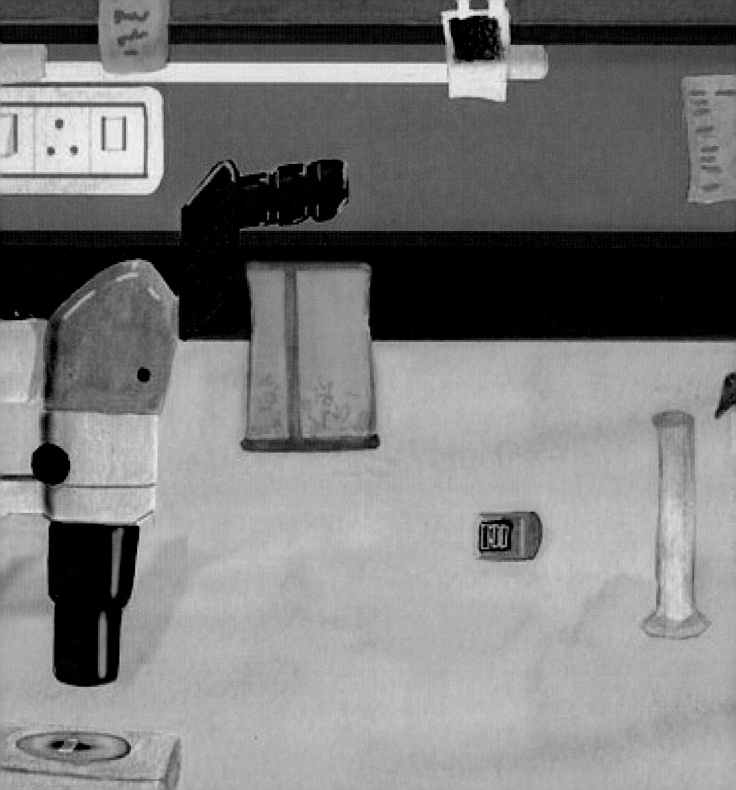

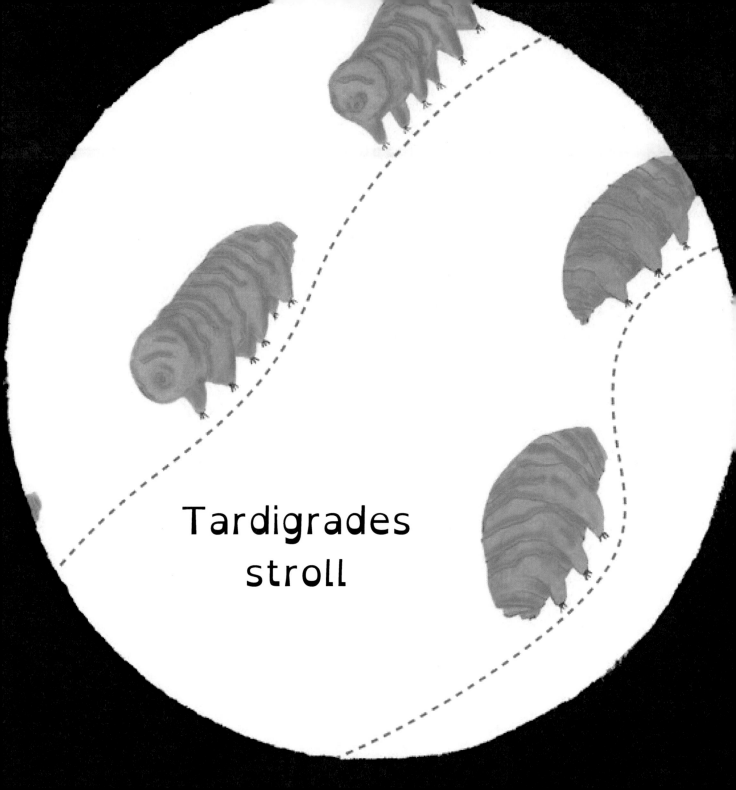

Tardigrades
stroll

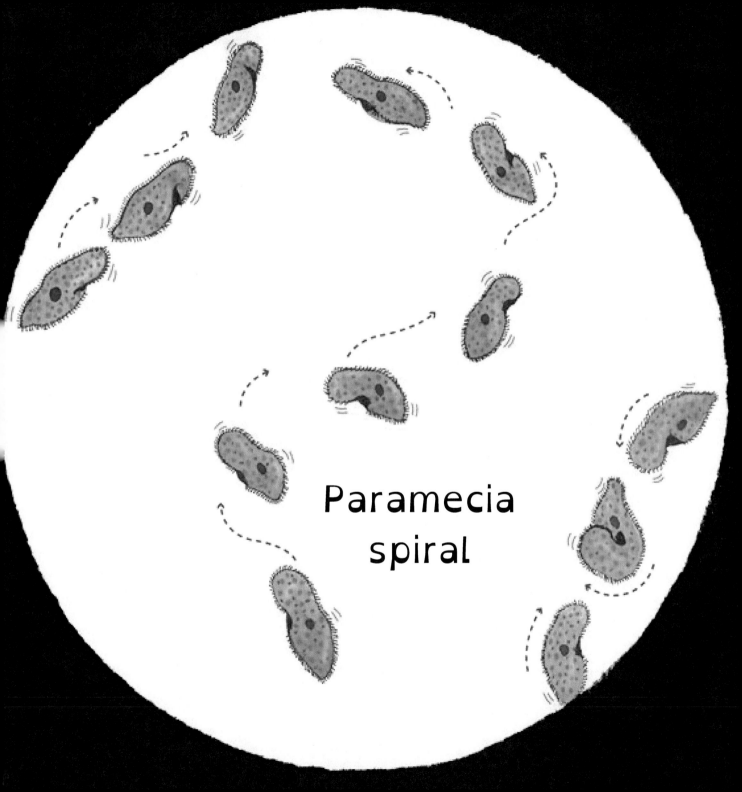

Paramecia
spiral

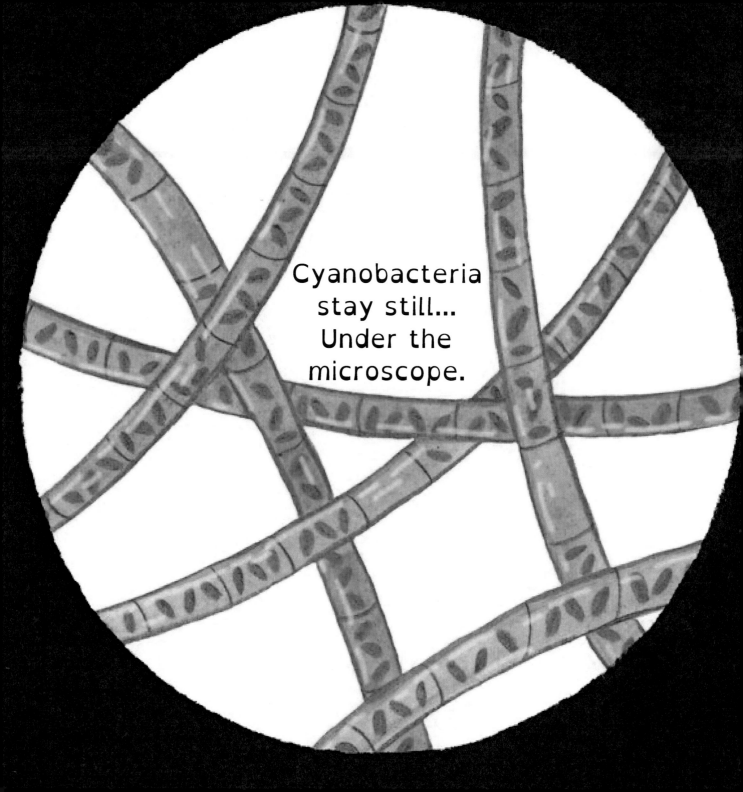

Microbes Are Everywhere!

Hydras look like plants, tardigrades walk like tiny bears and amoebas
are shapeshifters. But what they have in common is that they're all microbes, tiny creatures that live all around us.

From deep under the earth to far up in the sky, microbes are everywhere. They live in the freezing cold and in the bubbling heat.
They live in food, waste, rocks, trees, soil, and even you and me.

So how many microbes live around us? A drop of water from a pond
will have hundreds and hundreds of these tiny creatures! But to look
at them, we'll need to use a microscope. A microscope is a device
used to enlarge very small things that can't be seen with the naked eye.

Hydras can grow back
their lost body parts
and almost never die
of old age.

Euglenas, like plants,
can make their own
food through
photosynthesis.

If you cut a planaria into two, each
piece will develop
into an individual planaria.

Diatoms produce 25
to 40 percent of
the air we breathe.

Amoebas can change
their shapes.
Sometimes, they do
this to trap food.

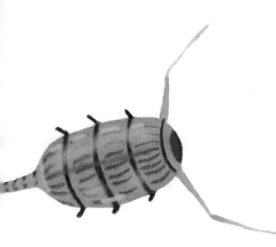

Tardigrades can survive in the most extreme conditions, like inside a volcano or in outer space.

A single copepod can eat thousands of diatoms in just 24 hours.

Cyanobacteria have been around for a very long time and have been found in fossils that are over a billion years old.

Paramecia swim really fast and can cover a distance of four times their length in a second.

Made in United States
North Haven, CT
23 April 2023

35794287R00015